MacKenzie Smiles, LLC
San Francisco, CA

www.mackenziesmiles.com

Originally published as *Slangen i Graset*
Copyright © Gyldendal Norsk Forlag AS 2007
[All rights reserved]
www.gyldendal.no

Author: Hans Sande
Illustrator: Gry Moursund

Translated by Tonje Vetleseter

Art production by Bernard Prinz

ISBN 978-0-9815761-0-7

Printed in China

10 9 8 7 6 5 4 3 2 1

Distributed in the U.S. and Canada by:
Ingram Publisher Services
One Ingram Blvd.
P.O. Box 3006
LaVergne, TN 37086
(888) 800-5978

Hans
Sande

Gry
Moursund

Translated by
Tonje Vetleseter

Snake
IN the
GRASS

MACKENZIE
SMILES
San Francisco

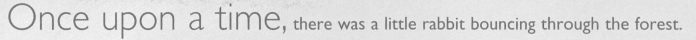

Once upon a time, there was a little rabbit bouncing through the forest.

What a lovely day! The sun was lovely, the forest was lovely, and

the rabbit was super lovely—yes, super-duper lovely.

So soft, and furry, and bouncy!

And smart—yes, super-duper smart.

The little rabbit jumped over a stream

without splashing the water. Then she

crawled under a barbed-wire fence

without tearing her fur, and

jumped into a garden.

Sniff, sniff. Lettuce!

And look there!

Super-duper carrots were lined up
and waiting for the rabbit!

One, two, three, four, seven, eight, ten…more than twenty in a row!

"Yum, yum! Just for me!" the rabbit laughed.

When she had eaten until she was nice and full, she jumped farther into the garden.

How nice and even the grass was!

All the blades were the same length!

Wonderfully good to roll around in!

"How great! Just for me!"
the rabbit laughed.

The little rabbit rolled and rolled in
the soft grass. I am the cutest rabbit
in the world, she thought. I have
never seen a rabbit with paws
as pretty, a tail as tufty, and
a stomach as stuffed.

Crunch, munch, lunch.

Look at me!

"Ye**sssss**, I see!" a green voice whispered.

Who was talking?

Suddenly the rabbit

discovered something

smooth slithering

through the grass.

A snake!

A long, slippery green snake!

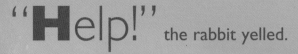

"**H**elp!" the rabbit yelled.

"**H**elp!" the snake yelled back.

"What? Do you need help?" asked the rabbit.

"Ye**ssss**, I have swallowed too much water," replied the snake.

"Are you pretending?"

"Ye**ssss**," the snake answered. "Do you like to pretend?"

"Yes, are you good at pretending?"

"I am good—yes, **ssss**uper good at pretending."

"Let's hear it, then!"

said the rabbit.

"But if I don't believe you,
I might bite you."

"OK," said the snake, "I am a cross-eyed cobra from Africa!"

"Yuck, you pretend badly!" cried the rabbit.

"It is true! Everyone in my family sees blurry.
Everyone uses gla**SSSSSSSSSS**es.
Even newborn snakes are born
with gla**SSSSSSSSSSSSS**es!"

"Yuck, you pretend badly, super-duper badly.
I'm going to bite you. Those glasses are just
ordinary sunglasses," said the rabbit.

"O**hhh**!" the snake said, surprised,
and took off the glasses.

The rabbit jumped up and bit the snake in the neck.

The snake spurted some water.

"Gulp!"

the snake splattered out.

"You are just an ordinary garden hose!"
the rabbit said, disappointed.

"No, no," the snake mumbled, "I am not ordinary."

"You are a completely ordinary, slippery garden hose
with a spout. And I am going to bite your tail off."

"O**hhh**, no! O**hhh**, no! Dear rabbit, wait a minute.
Can I have another chance?"

"OK," said the little rabbit.

"Let me go, then!" said the snake.

The rabbit let the snake go.

He curled up and said in a raspy voice,

"I am a **rrr**rattlesnake from the Amazon."

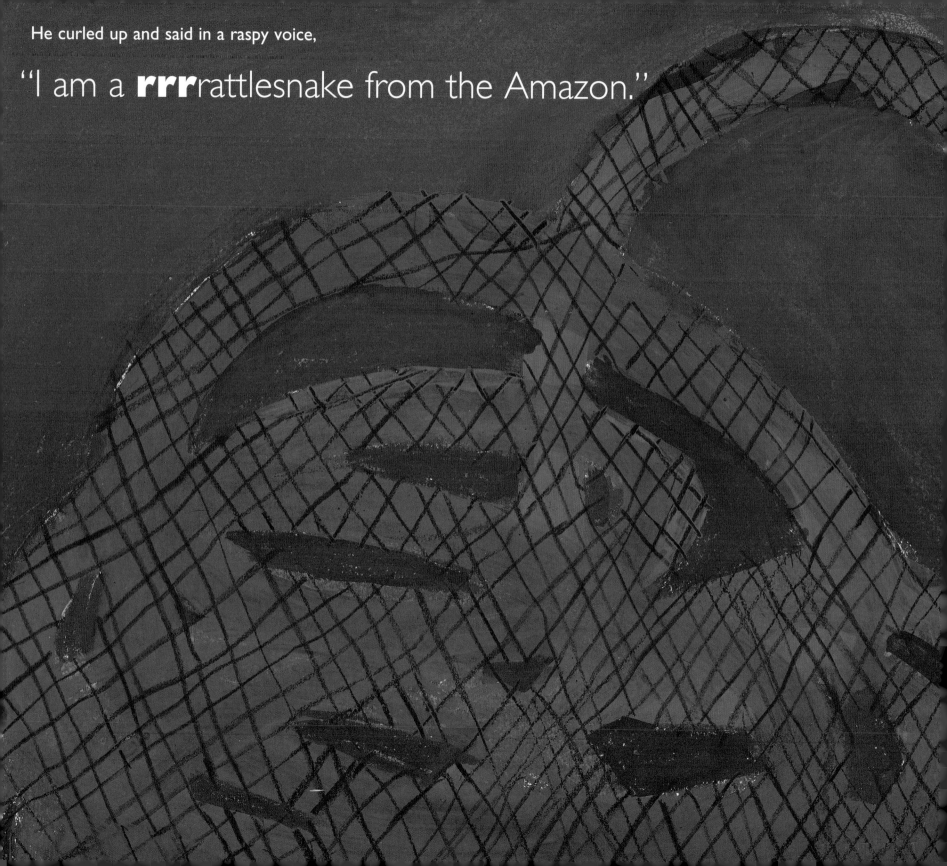

"Is that true? You're not pretending?" asked the rabbit.

Rrrrr**r**rrrrrrrrrrrr! ^{The tail rattled.}

"Oh, my! How scary!

How can you rattle like that with your tail?

And the Amazon? Where is that?"

'Come with me. You will **ssssss**ee."

Under the roots of a tree, there was a hole,

a black little hole in the ground.

The snake slithered in, and the rabbit

crawled after him. They crawled through

a long, dark tunnel. It became narrower and

narrower. The rabbit couldn't see anything.

She could barely breathe. She crawled and crawled,

with dirt in her eyes and dirt in her nose.

"It is itchy! I want to turn around!"

the rabbit whimpered.

But it was too late to go back. There was no room to turn around.

The rabbit had to dry her tears and keep going in the dark.

Ahead she could hear the rattling from the rattlesnake's tail.

Rrrrrrrrrrrr!

"I am tired!" the rabbit complained.

The rattlesnake just rattled on. Farther than far, they crawled for many hours. Wasn't it evening and bedtime soon? Soon Daddy Rabbit would come and sing a lullaby!

"I am small!" the rabbit whined.

"**Rrrrrrrrrrrrrrr!** You are tired and you are small, but you can get through this one last crawl!" the snake rattled, and slithered on.

"Mommy, Daddy, Grandpa!" the rabbit cried. "I want to go home."

Then suddenly the tunnel widened out. Fresh air flowed to the rabbit.

Yippee! The rabbit jumped up next to the snake and out into the open air.

Look! Juicy green leaves, big as umbrellas.

Listen! Chirping songs from a thousand birds.

Smell! Spicy cinnamon and sweet bananas.

This was a whole jungle, a wet, green, and dark rain forest!

"You pretend really well!" the rabbit said.

"Yes, I did say I was **sssss**uper good."

"Such a lovely forest before us! Super lovely, super-duper lovely. But a little scary."

"Ye**ssssssss**, isn't it? This is the Amazon!" said the snake,
and coiled himself around a thick branch.

"You pretend really well!" The little rabbit was shaking.
"The rain forest must be full of wild animals."

"Ju**SSS**st monkeys," said the snake.

"Dangerous monkeys?" asked the rabbit.

"Ju**SSS**st leopards," said the snake.

"Dangerous leopards?" asked the rabbit.

"Ju**SSS**st crocodiles," said the snake.

"Don't tell me about such scary animals," said the rabbit.
"Where are the other rabbits?

Where are Bugs Bunny,
Peter Rabbit,
and the Easter Bunny?"

"Now you are being **rrrr**really silly.
Those rabbits don't exist here!"

"There are no rabbits here?"

"Not anymore. But don't be afraid. I will look after you.
Do you want to come home and meet my family?
You can **SSSSS**leep over."

"Oh yes, I do. I want to say night-night
and go to sleep. I am so tired."

"**Ssss**sit on my back,"
the snake said, and
the rabbit jumped up.

The snake slithered quickly along the forest floor.

"You are so fast and strong!" said the rabbit. "I am looking forward to getting there! But who will sing me a lullaby?"

"Great-grandma can do that," the snake answered.
"She can sing **Rrr**rrrrr, **rrr**rrrrrr, snakess**ssr**rrrrrr."

"But your great-grandmother—isn't she a snake? And your family—isn't it a snake family?"

"Ye**ssss**, of course! Did you think my dad was a **sss**snail and my mother a rubber band?"

"No, but don't real snakes eat live rabbits? That is what my mother says!"

"You mustn't li**sss**ten to grown-ups!

You are my friend, aren't you?

You are my be**sss**st friend.

Come and give me a hug.

M**MMm**mmmm.

No one is allowed to eat you."

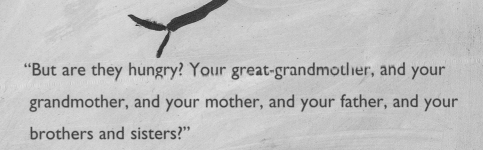

"But are they hungry? Your great-grandmother, and your grandmother, and your mother, and your father, and your brothers and sisters?"

"I don't know if they are hungry, I haven't been home in many years."

"Is that true?"

"Yes, it is true, it is **SSSSSSS**uper true," the snake answered, and slithered through the rain forest.

At long last, he slowed down and curled up on a large, flat stone.

The full moon shone down on the snake and the little rabbit.

"Are we there?" the rabbit asked.

"**Kss**ss**S**sssssssssh!" said the snake.

"What do you mean, Kssssssh?" asked the rabbit.

"It is **SSSSS**nake language," said the snake.

Kssss**S**ssssssssh!

In an instant, the whole forest came alive.

Snakes came dangling down from every tree.

Small snakes, big snakes, fat snakes, thin snakes, spotted snakes, and stripy snakes.

And a fat, black snake came
gliding out of the darkness,
as long and dark as the night itself.

The fat, black snake slithered onto the flat stone, and bumped into the green snake.

Ksssssss **k**sssss **k**sssssssss!
Mamma mia!

"**Kaka**ka? Is that you, my little cucumber?"

the fat, black snake asked, and pressed herself close to him.

"How big you have grown! Where have you been all these years?"

"I have been to America," the snake answered.

"And guess who I have brought for dinner? My new friend!"

"A viper?" asked his mother. "Or an adder?"

"No, a rabbit!"

"**Ra-ra**-ra-rabbit? Alive?"

"Oh ye**sss**s, bright-eyed
and bushy-tailed."

'But **whe**-whe-where do you have that divine
bright-eyed and bushy-tailed **ra-ra**-ra-rabbit?''
Here in the middle!'' said the snake, and uncoiled.

In the middle, the little rabbit sat shaking, surrounded by hundreds of hungry snakes. Rattlesnakes and boa constrictors, apple snakes, cobras, and rolling snakes. The rolling snakes bit their tails, then rolled like wheels. Oh, a whole rhumba of poisonous rolling snakes came rolling out and stopped abruptly in front of the rabbit. Oh, how they stared with their yellow eyes, swinging backward and forward, and how their tongues whirled and swirled in the air.

Mmmmmm! We smell rabbit!"

"Look at that delicious little bunny rabbit!"

"Dear little dinner guest! Come here! Let us **SSS**scold you."

"**Ss**scold you! **Ss**scold you!" cried all small and big snakes, all fat and thin snakes, all long and short snakes, all the yellow and green and black and red snakes.

"**Ss**scold you!"
"**Ss**scold you!"

"But why do they want to scold me?
What have I done wrong?"

"No, no, we are not going to scold you!
We want to **hh**hold, **hh**hold, hold you!"

Oh, come here, come here, you cute, you furry, you **sss**super-delicious rabbit.

The snakes came closer and closer. The rabbit shook in her fur, and pushed the green snake.

"Help! Help! You must not let them eat me," the rabbit whispered. "You are my best friend."

"What can I do?" the green snake asked.

"You have to pretend!
Pretend something clever before it is too late."

"OK," said the snake. "Lisssssssten, everybody!
I am only an ordinary garden hose with a spout."

"And your family—what about them? Say it quickly!" begged the rabbit.

"My whole family is at the beach on the river down there behind the ga**SSS**s station."

"And all the other scary snakes?"

"They are just cucumber**SSS** hanging in the greenhouse over there."

"And the rolling snakes?"

"They are on a bike trip to California."

"Now you pretended super well, super-duper well!" said the rabbit, and kissed the snake on his spout.

The rabbit was happy, as super-duper happy as a free, bright-eyed, bushy-tailed little rabbit could be.

She swallowed some water and pulled a carrot out of the ground. Evening had come to the garden.

Moonlight! But the moon was not as round and beautiful as the one in the Amazon.

The moon was hurt!

"Oh, the moon is sick!"
the rabbit complained.
The rabbit ate another carrot and
looked up at the poor moon.

It was completely quiet
in the garden.

No, hush!

Thump,
thump,
thump!

From behind the red currant bushes, Daddy Rabbit came jumping.

"Where have you been? It is dark, and it is bedtime, and we have been looking for you!"

"I have been to the Amazon, to the rain forest, together with my new friend, the garden hose."

"What? In the Amazon? In the rain forest? Together with the garden hose? You pretend well, little rabbit!"

"Yes, do you like it, Daddy? I have become such a good pretender. Super-duper good. Do you want to hear?"

"Oh yes, tell me all about it while we hop home."

"But Daddy, have you seen the moon? He is hurt, very sick."

"Yes, you are right. He doesn't look too well."

"Daddy, you can fix the moon, can't you?"

"Oh yes, but I need a couple of weeks for the job. A little work every night, and then the moon will be round and whole again."

"Great, Daddy! You can fix everything."

And then they hopped home while the little rabbit told her story. High above them, the half-moon hung on Its nail with a lopsided smile and, down in the grass, the garden hose slept with green-snake dreams.